AF445113

LIVING IN HELL
WHILE DRINKING ICE WATER

RIVIERA LAUREN

Living In Hell While Drinking Ice Water

Copyright © 2023 Riviera Lauren

All Rights Reserved.

Manufactured in the United States of America.

All rights reserved. No part of this book may be used or reproduced in any capacity without written permission except in the case of brief quotations intended for use in critical articles and reviews.

In the event that you use or enact any of the material in this book, the author and publisher assume no responsibility for your actions.

The publisher, Lightning Fast Book Publishing, assumes no responsibility for any content presented in this book.

Summary: Living In Hell While Drinking Ice Water is a work of inspirational fiction, that takes the reader on a journey from extreme life adversity to triumph and overcoming.

ISBN: 979-8-9882743-8-4

CONTENTS

FOREWORD

Like most of us, Riviera Lauren is a complex person who has been forged by her experiences and her inherited temperament. In Riviera Lauren's case, her experiences have their roots in rural Mississippi. Riviera Lauren courageously shares many personal stories that document the various forms of depravity and poverty, and just as many that highlight hope and forgiveness. As one hears Riviera Lauren recount her experiences, they will soon begin to learn how she, like most of us, grows to become complex individuals with seeming confusing and juxtaposed characteristics. Riviera Lauren is bright and strong like a diamond; and beautiful and delicate like a Magnolia flower, which one might find in her home state of Mississippi. She is an amalgam of many complex life experiences. Many toxic and many life giving. If one opens their hearts and minds and listens to her story they will be entertained, and more importantly strengthen their hope and be inspired to grow into a positive light - like Riviera Lauren's.

Christopher Bir, M.D.

Acknowledgements

Almighty God - All Praises, Glory, and Credit Given to You.

Given this is a work of anonymity, I am not willfully excluding those who have been instrumental to my life's growth and ascension. If you know me, you know who you are, and that I have the deepest reverence and appreciation for you.

You are loved.

Riviera Lauren

An Open Letter to My Mother

Dear Mom,

I want to take a moment to express my love and appreciation for you. As a Black woman in the south, and mother, you faced challenges and overcame obstacles that I can never truly understand. But despite the struggles you may have faced, you have always been a source of strength, love, and guidance in my life.

From a young age, you instilled in me the importance of family, community, and education. You have taught me the value of hard work, determination, and perseverance. And through your actions, you have shown me what it truly means to be a loving and caring parent.

Your unwavering love and support have been a constant source of comfort in my life. You have always been there to pick me up when I fell, to listen when I needed someone to talk to, and to offer your sage advice when I faced difficult decisions.

Your patience, kindness, and understanding have never faltered, even when I may have been at my worst.

Beyond your endless support, you possess an array of positive motherly attributes that I am grateful to have experienced throughout my life. Your generosity is unmatched. You give without hesitation, and you always put the needs of others before your own. Whether it's taking care of a sick family member, lending a listening ear to a friend in need, or volunteering your time to help others, your heart knows no bounds.

Your strength is another admirable trait that has always inspired me. You have overcome numerous obstacles in your life and never allowed them to hold you back. You have shown me that with hard work and determination, anything is possible. I admire your resilience and how you always face challenges with grace and determination.

Your creativity is also a quality that has always impressed me. You have a natural gift for art and music, and your passion for expression is contagious. I remember spending hours drawing and painting with you, and how you always encouraged me to explore my own creativity. You have a unique ability to make even the most mundane tasks enjoyable, and your infectious sense of humor always brightens the mood.

Lastly, I want to express my deep appreciation for your culinary talents. Your cooking is truly one of a kind. I remember the aroma of your homemade soul food filling our home and my heart with warmth and joy. Every bite of your food is infused with love and care, and I can never get enough of it. Your macaroni and cheese is the stuff of legends, and your fried chicken could give any restaurant a run for its' money. The way you put your heart and soul into every dish you make is a testament to your dedication as a mother and your commitment to our family.

Thank you for sharing your talents with us and for being such an amazing mother. You are a true inspiration to me, and I am grateful for every moment we have shared together. I feel incredibly blessed to have grown up with such a talented and caring mother, and I know that your love and guidance will continue to be a cherished part of my life for years to come.

With all my love and gratitude,

Riviera Lauren

A Thank You to My Friends and Family

You have my deepest apologies if you are not listed here and do not have mention. Thank you. I still value everyone who has been part of my network, and made my dream of writing a book become a reality. Please let me know once you're on me and I'll be sure you're mentioned in my next book.

"Then you will know the truth, and truth will set you free" **(John 8:32).**

Many of my loyal, loving and devoted friends ask me: why did I leave living in a 12,000 Sq. Ft. mansion on 12+ acre with a pool and pond located in Ashburn, VA?

Easy answer: I discovered there are things in life which money simply cannot buy. It made my daughter and I miserable, and I am working hard every day of my life correcting my mistakes as a parent in my relationship with her. It's a work in progress, and she's my heart.

I love you, Blair.

There have been many days where I could only feel sorry for myself with no strength nor power to get through another day. I had zero fight in me. I felt as a mother if I was living in hell. Thank God, he never gave up on me. I had forgotten how to stop feeling sorry for myself. During that time, my spine was in non stop chronic pain for years.

Damaged nerve roots in the cervical spine and neck which led to permanent damage, causing a change in my neurological function. The neurological deficits, such as numbness, altered reflexes, weakness, radiate from the neck into the shoulder, arm, hand, and fingers. Pins-and-needles tingling and/or pain, which range from achy to shock-like or burning, also radiate down into the arm and/or hand. I couldn't even sleep without pain.

I was physically injured after a New Year's Eve Party in 2017. Left in a pool of blood, I was injured so badly inside the front portion of both eyes between the clear cornea and the colored iris. I experienced changes in vision, dizziness, headaches, and sensitivity to light. As a result, I struggled to leave the house for weeks. I couldn't develop the courage to look at myself in the mirror for fear of seeing visible bleeding in the white of the eye.

As a loyal and devoted wife, I always made up lies of what truly happened to me.

Due to the spinal trauma injury, it was eventually medically necessary for me to receive artificial disk replacement surgery.

This was the only way I could recover, and develop independence from the monthly neck and shoulder injections, daily medication, weekly massage, and physical therapy. None of which actually provided the level of pain relief I needed. I felt useless as a person. Two artificial disks were placed in my spine. I would never wish that on my worst enemy nor the devil himself.

A deep sense of fear gripped me: balancing my obligations as mother, dealing with the tremendous responsibilities I have at work, and ongoing physical abuse hitting me all at one time. I kept putting the surgery off because I was so stressed and knew that I would have a stroke or heart attack during the surgery. I had no other choice on the day I lost complete feeling in my entire upper body.

My daughter Blair was 12 years old; she called 911 for help, and a very close friend to make proper care arrangements for her. Blair was my savior; she was so brave and calm through the entire time. I thank God each day for blessing me with her. I have told you these things, so that in me you may have peace. In this world you will have trouble. But take heart! I have overcome the world." (John 16:33).

INTRODUCTION

The remainder of this book is a complete work of fiction. It is written from the perspective of a mythical woman named Riviera Lauren. Any connection it may have to real life events, or events in my life is entirely coincidental. Nothing in this book should be taken as fact.

Anyone with limited time, especially working single parents; I appreciate the costly devotion of your limited and valuable time to reading my life story.

Living in Hell While Drinking Ice Water is written to have a propensity for another matter of the heart, forgiveness. I also mean no harm nor disrespect to my parents, relatives, or friends.

Chapter 1
<hr>

RIVIERA'S CHAPTER

What can I say, outside of being born and raised in Pela-hatchie, Mississippi? I'm a humble woman.

The youngest of an older brother and sister, this taught me how to communicate effectively and learning from older people, somewhat prepared me for life. At the age of 13, I decided boarding school was my only lifeline to success. Trauma is a bitch, and is undeniable. How you grow up in life can forever dictate your future, but I was determined to not let that happen.

Where should I begin? Unfortunately, the KKK is still active and marches proudly in Mississippi. I guess time somewhat doesn't change. The old saying still exists with the railroad tracks and division with race. Whites live on a side of town, while blacks live on the complete opposite side of town. As a female, it is truly oppressive growing up with limited options as a minority. The only hope was to marry outside of your family; not your second cousin.

My Mother Did the Best She Could with What She Knew

There's only so far you can rise above your own upbringing. My father was unable to be present and active in my life. This gave me generational trauma, a curse that I vow to break within my lifetime. She was raped constantly for years by her Step Father while her mother was well aware. Which is still baffling, as long as her step father never cheated outside of the family, her mom was perfectly fine.

Eventually my mother was able to escape the continued abuse from her step father, she eventually left for no return wearing multiple jeans on countless nights. As long as his pickle remained in the family. Grandma said it was kosher. When he steps out, a bullet awaits his name.

Of little surprise, my mother conceived at an early age with my brother. Geography is Destiny, and history repeats itself. My brother was taken away at an early age due to abuse. Pure and innocent, my brother walked in on our mother and her partner, visually exposed to trauma, and lacking adult understanding of sex, and assumed that someone was causing pain to our mother. He immediately picked up a vase and cracked it over the gentleman's head for protection of our mother.

Our mom used corporal punishment. But in this situation, she overused it. Disciplining my brother so badly that the school reached out to CPS for abuse. After finding undeniable marks and strikes on his body. My brother was sent to live with my grandmother and (also) perverted husband for the time being.

Incest is quite common in the south. While kept hush hush, only to be discussed within the family, sexual abuse in some form is quite common. And if you speak up, or ask for outside help, you will be the outcast of the entire family. This is how it all began.

Long-Term Effect of Police Brutality in BIOPC Community

Please help & imagine this...

Devoted-loyal, but disabled African American Female Veteran resting in her bed; and the police entering your bedroom while half dressed. Interrogated in your own bed within five minutes handcuffs are being placed on you. You have no underwear on in front of three white male police.

Imagine your rights are never read and the reason for your arrest is completely withheld.

This happened to me in the dead of winter. I was thrown like a lamb to slaughter, naked, afraid, and completely and unknowingly, into the back of a police car without shoes or even a loosely knit sweater to protect me from the bitter cold. Without heat in the back of a police car, I accepted my fate in that cabin of the police cruiser.

To Anyone
Who will Hear My Cry;

I am devastated and traumatized from the events that transpired on the night of my arrest.

The police were called to our home in the middle of the night on a domestic violence call. My husband answered the door and he was briefly questioned. At some point a white female officer did appear, waking me with a bombardment of overwhelming questions.

In the blink of an eye, 3 caucasian male officers were also in my bedroom. Nevertheless, several additional police officers appeared at my home.

I repeatedly asked the officers to provide my husband in the room to secure the truth of the events that were unfolding.

After the barrage of questioning in an indecent manner, I was dragged out of my bed and handcuffed with no undergarments on with a tee shirt that obviously did not cover my vagina. The comforter set from the bed could have been applied to shield my private part.

Before placing me in the police vehicle, I was asked if I had pants and the officers put my pants on with my handcuffs on at my front door after the embarrassment of already being exposed.

I was never read my miranda rights or told why I was being arrested. I was ushered to the police car with no shoes on in the dead of winter, and left in the back of the police car with no heat, while the police officers were outside discussing their plans for the weekend.

Flash forward to 6 months of court and physical pain, all without my daughter. I endured massive legal fees, and suffering defamation of character, embarrassment to all while affecting my career as one of the few Black Women CEO Veteran owned IT companies in the US which is something that I spent a lifetime building with others to achieve.

Now imagine if this was your mom, daughter, niece, or sister; anyone you love that is a woman. This might not sound important to some, but I have to stand up, share my testimony and make sure that this NEVER happens to anyone else.

The aftermath is the destruction of trust that I have lost for the people who are supposed to protect, serve, and keep us all safe is destroyed.

The Loudoun County police were negligent in my arrest. Again, I was never given my constitutional right to first know why I was being arrested. There was indecent exposure while being groped with no underwear, and afterwards being arrested in winter weather with no shoes and then thrown into jail.

Again, I seek Justice. Perhaps my testimony can help change/ adapt a law or policy on the due process for how to conduct an arrest where a naked connect female/male is being arrested.

I appreciate your time and support in my testimony and in the hope of making this a better and safer world. May justice be served.

My deepest sorrow goes out to the other voices who will not be heard. Those who are unable to stand up and fight back.

Limitation of the Law
to Protect Abused Family

Someone has to die for the legal system to become effective in the Commonwealth of Virginia. I forgot my values while finding myself immobilized. I felt cursed from my family's previous history of actions or not having the awareness of the sins that were committed in life.

Being raped by your own husband and not knowing how to tell anyone was devastating and embarrassing. Divulging that information was not possible since I didn't know how. Who do you tell? As of this day, I do have the answer: report it and never be ashamed.

I was praying and hoping that I wasn't pregnant. My life was already miserable enough so adding a second baby to the equation was not an option.

I was raised to know that I shouldn't ever fight a man; I tried and failed painfully after I was punched in the face by my ex-spouse. He could never touch me intimately ever again. Sex was no longer of a service and therapy couldn't help me since I wasn't 100% honest during the sessions regarding the physical abuse. By no means necessary, I'm not perfect, and only use words to hurt as a defense mechanism without using my fist. This behavior is too unacceptable.

Financial Abuse of
the Legal System

Health is real money. I never told anyone throughout my marriage of the abuse. Bosom friends knew or shall I say had an idea. They at no time overstepped, but only asked questions never making statements or expressions for me to leave my ex-spouse. My soul, mind, and spirit did not permit me to speak negatively to others of what my daughter and I experienced in life until I was able to no longer live in that nightmarish hostile situation.

I made several attempts prior to my arrest for an amicable peaceful separation. I even offered to pay off one bill to allow for him and our daughter to live within close proximity of us both for frequent weekly visits to both parents' residence. I also offered to remain as business partners even though the marriage didn't work out. He would agree at that moment and later that day, change his mind to disagree.

He has never agreed to anything with me. I can't afford to just give him funds while paying all of the legal bills. Any payment my Ex shall receive from me is only for Blair.

As a result of paying for the following legal expenses from 2019 - Present :

Criminal Court - Attorney Fees Mediation - Attorney & Judge Fees Arbitration - Attorney & Judge Fees Restraining

Order Hearing - Attorney Fees Business Attorney Fees Forensic Accountant Fees Ex-Spouse's Attorney Fees

I wanted to make it well aware that there are a total of 11+ Attorneys. I'm currently at my limit with litigation to just let it be known. I was required to attend court once or twice a month within a 6 month period. Funds that could have been invested in our daughter were applied to legal expenses. As of today, I'm still dealing with litigation and am too ashamed to share the total amount. I've reached out to the Ex directly begging to please stop wasting money, and his response was, "just do what I tell you to do" and "This is your punishment for wanting out of the marriage."

I have voiced all of my concerns every step of the way. Just in case, all attorneys are aware that I can depict my frustration at times with the massive financial hardships; even though I don't want to ever express myself in such a way. It should be a crime to abuse and waste court system's time for falsifying evidence, perjury, and for someone's own personal gain.

The Struggle to be Proven Innocent Until Being Proven Guilty

The ex-spouse verbal and physical abuse was repeatedly practiced in secret or when no one was around. In my family's defense, I never told anyone of the physical abuse. It seems that my Stepdad, Mom, and Sister were so disappointed in me for no longer wanting to be in an abusive relationship. I would receive calls that I needed to come home and return back to my ex-spouse. I was so exhausted from being told to remain in an abusive marriage that was going to kill me. This issue went on for years while I was secretly screaming for help. I was frustrated with this problem from every angle of my life. My ex-spouse knew that I would never share family private business, and that was used against me. He would find other ways to manipulate and try to isolate all of my relationships.

In a million years, I would have never imagined logs of any or all forms of communication, videos, pictures, etc required to be generated to prove my innocence in the court of law. As of now, I still have understandable concerns about communicating directly with him due to threats of incarceration and past history of my arrest.

Powerless While Dealing
with Obsession

Just to reassure myself in my marriage that I exhausted all options, I asked my ex-spouse how I could make him happy. His response was to have sex every day. I said OKAY, he didn't last a half of week, and treated me the same during the entire time. At least I can say that I gave it 100% and tried. I knew that I wasn't the issue, and I could not make him happy.

It wouldn't be fair to write all about the pain and never mention the pleasure. In the darkest days of my life, then come Oooo's, as in multiple ways I could never imagine. Why and How did I miss out? Holla if you hear me or anyway relatable. I was looking for a scratch for an itch after my divorce since I've always had to endure sex.

In spite of what preceded, authentic love for myself was mandatory to allow me the opportunity to experience stunning everlasting passion and hope for my future lover. True Love making nor any romantic connection would have been impossible in my mind, space, or environment to ever enjoy without loving myself first.

Revolving Everything that I Built to Protect My Child

You could give a child the world, something that you or I never received. Will they ever appreciate it? I've learned not to. We all want more for our kids' sake. However, not knowing what comes along with this from any race. Trust funds and generational wealth babies are such a passion of mine, but they can be pacified, while being set up for failure since all is given. When a child witnesses abuse consistently that looks normal to anyone, how will they know that's not okay or realistic? As a parent we do our best; it doesn't mean it's right. Providing our love, time, and attention is a great start in the best direction.

On several attempts the ex-spouse has denied visitation rights and communication with our daughter even with the request of his supervision. I have always encouraged a healthy positive relationship with them both since tomorrow is not promised. I will never want our child to hate me for not allowing her to have a relationship with her father. I continue to pray for the same in return.

Silence & Stress Almost Destroyed Me
& Gave My Abuser the Power

Silence was used against me in the worst ways possible. The first time I was raped, I could never forget. I left the baby-sitter's home with my mom, not knowing how to feel as a child. Please keep in mind that my mom was working non-stop to make ends meet financially. My pops and mom did not have the best relationship, so he wasn't around - without any disrespect against him. When we arrived home, I was told to take a bath. My toot toot was so inflamed. As a child, I was doubtful to tell my mom what happened to me. I didn't know how to say it because I was lost for words. While in the tub she asked me, did I sleep with a little boy. I was afraid and knew then I couldn't say anything. No child should never carry that burden. While mom was working after hours, I was left alone quite a bit under the watch of my sister which allowed me full access to erotic obscene sexual videos. Thank God, I was able to not allow that to obtain the best of me.

My ex-spouse and I attended marriage counseling throughout the marriage to address accusations of me having an affair with a woman and man; the Ex deliberately forged my signature for loans, placing a max on my credit cards without my knowledge, and I discovered this when I attempted to make a purchase that was unsuccessful. Humiliation at it's finest since our accounts were combined while making the exact same salary.

How do we learn healthy communication with our kids since I'm too guilty of lacking? Listen, pay attention, honesty, and transparency.

What Could I Have
Done Differently?

I was never honest with myself before. Only checking a box at a time in my life, I could never be seen for my hard work and accomplishments without my Spouse. Since I didn't know any better, I was absolutely okay being a supportive wife without any recognition with him taking all of the credit. In my mind we were a team, while he didn't see it this way. What's mine is his and what's his is mine; old school mentally. I was sadly mistaken and enlightened that was never his agenda. You live and you learn.

I had a heart of giving to everyone and even pushing individuals that didn't want to be pushed. I was never a selfish person and put no demands on anyone. There's enough success for us all out there. I knew it took an Army or massive team to build generational worth. I wanted that, but not knowing at what expense.

The one thing that my ex-spouse loved about me initially when we met, is the one thing he hates the most about me. There's so much more for me to give and accomplish to be a Blessing to others. I pray to God for the spirit of discernment, and for God to use me to be a Blessing to others. As a child, I prayed non-stop for that Blessing. Be careful what you ask for in life, but I knew that was my calling. I love giving back to the needy and not the greedy. However, I do understand you have to give or invest in something in order to make something.

Pushing my spouse to success without any knowledge developed into hate for me of no return with statements from him, "can't you stop wanting more, why are you so driven, and are you that greedy?" I had no response, but only I married you without any credentials, and knowing your cousin was your roommate. Since I was such a classic overachiever in life, he felt that he had no choice nor intentions to ever be a supportive lover in return for my professional and personal goals. I had only one role which was to never have a voice, have no career with a Master degree while striving for a Doctorate degree from John Hopkins, and a one-sided marriage in his favor.

Prior to the marriage, we never had the discussion of having any kids. Premarital counseling would have been of much value. After the first year of being married, The Ex gave me an ultimatum that either I have a baby or the marriage was over. Years later, he told our daughter that I never wanted her while we were all in the kitchen. Without any hesitation, I immediately explained to Blair that I didn't want any kids at first, but ever since she has been in my life, she has been my everything, and God sent me a blessing to make me the woman that I am today. If I had to do it all over, I would and she means the world to me. Maybe that wasn't the best answer or response for her at that time, but it was my truth and honest answer. I'm not by any means perfect, but I love being a mom with an open mind to learn and always strive for improvement.

How Do I Still
Overcome It All?

God, friends, & family is how I was able to overcome it all. I walked away giving my ex-spouse it all and that still wasn't enough. I witnessed that he wanted my blood while praying and hoping that wouldn't bring any harm his way even if we weren't a match. He never cared.

I've learned to put myself first. I can't help anyone if I'm not okay. Please know that vision, drive, and love is still there and of provision that's alive for like-minded individuals requesting support.

He would always apologize for all the pain he put me through. What I could never understand until now was why he wanted to break me and call me a devil worshiper for participating in positive organizations within the community. It all made sense that I wasn't what he wanted. My ambition in life agitated him. It became a competition for him, and a moment of bashing and degrading me as a mom, wife, and human being for wanting so much more in life while helping others. This is fulfilling to my spirit and heart.

Riviera Lauren

About the Author

Riviera Lauren is a proud mother, very accomplished athlete, and record breaking business woman. She is a representation of everything presented in this work of fiction. Extreme adversity was her reality growing up, and followed her into adulthood. Riviera chose to be a perpetual overcomer, and speaks to the overcomer in every reader of her books.

www.ingramcontent.com/pod-product-compliance
Lightning Source LLC
Chambersburg PA
CBHW051335150726
47997CB00004B/1476